The Petal Fairies

For Laura Rouffiac,
who loves fairies (and bunnies!)

Special thanks to
Narinder Dhami

ORCHARD BOOKS
338 Euston Road, London NW1 3BH
Orchard Books Australia
Level 17/207 Kent Street, Sydney, NSW 2000
A Paperback Original

HiT entertainment

First published in 2007 by Orchard Books
Rainbow Magic is a registered trademark of Working Partners Limited.
Series created by Working Partners Limited, London W6 0QT

A CIP catalogue record for this book is available
from the British Library.

ISBN 978 1 84616 461 3
3 5 7 9 10 8 6 4 2

Printed and bound in China by Imago

Orchard Books is a division of Hachette Children's Books

www.orchardbooks.co.uk

Olivia
the Orchid
Fairy

by Daisy Meadows

ORCHARD BOOKS

www.rainbowmagic.co.uk

The Fairyland Palace

Blossom Hall

Fairy Garden

Leafley Village

Visitors' Centre

I need the magic petals' powers,
To give my castle garden flowers.
And so I use my magic well
To work against the fairies' spell.

From my wand ice magic flies,
Frosty bolt through fairy skies.
And this crafty spell I weave
To bring the petals back to me.

Contents

"Welcome to Rainbow Falls Gardens,"
said the man behind the desk, passing
tickets and a map over the counter.
"I hope you enjoy your day!"

Kirsty Tate smiled at her friend Rachel
Walker as their parents thanked the man
and picked up the tickets. Then the two
families set off through the grand

wrought-iron gates that stood at the
entrance to the gardens. The Tates and
the Walkers were spending the Easter
holidays together, and so far they'd been
having a magical time. Kirsty and
Rachel hoped today would be just
as exciting.

As they walked through the gates,
the girls found themselves at the edge of
a large grassy lawn, with a copse of trees
at the far end. The sun was warm on
their faces, and they could hear
birds singing.

"Let's see," Mr Walker said, opening up the map. "Where shall we go first?"

Rachel, Kirsty and Mr Walker looked at the map. There was an orchid garden, an arboretum and, of course, the famous Rainbow Falls.

"I want to see the waterfall first," Rachel said eagerly.

"Ah," said Mr Walker. "I was just about to suggest the arboretum."

"What's an arboretum?" Kirsty asked.

"It's an area with lots of beautiful trees and shrubs," her dad told her, coming over to look at the map too.

"Woof!" said Buttons, the Walkers'

dog, pulling hard on his lead.

"I think Buttons fancies the arboretum, as well," Mrs Walker laughed.

"I think I'd like to see the falls," Kirsty said. "Can we go there and meet you at the arboretum afterwards?" she asked her parents.

"I don't see why not," Mr Tate agreed.

"We'll see you at the entrance to the arboretum in an hour," Mrs Tate told the girls. Then she frowned slightly as she glanced at the nearby flowerbeds. "I hope the trees in the arboretum are healthier than these flowers," she said. "Look, half of them are drooping, or dead!"

Rachel and Kirsty
exchanged glances.
They knew exactly
why the flowers
didn't look as
beautiful as they
should. Unknown to
their parents, the girls were
secret friends with the fairies and often
helped them when they were in trouble.
This time, they were helping the Petal
Fairies find their missing magic petals.
The petals made flowers bloom and
grow beautifully in Fairyland and in the
human world, so while the petals were
missing, flowers all over the world were
wilting and dying.

"I hope we find one of the petals
today," Kirsty whispered to Rachel.

"These flowers really need a bit of fairy magic!"

"Definitely," Rachel agreed.

The fairies had shown the girls how cruel Jack Frost had sent his goblin servants to steal all seven magic petals from Fairyland. He wanted the petals so that he could make flowers grow in the freezing gardens around his Ice Castle. But when Jack Frost's icy magic had collided with the Petal Fairies' own spell to get their petals back, the seven petals had been caught up in a huge magic explosion that had sent them flying into the human world.

Kirsty and Rachel had already helped the Petal Fairies find the Tulip Petal, the Poppy Petal, the Lily Petal and the Sunflower Petal, but there were still three

lost petals left to find. And the girls knew
that Jack Frost's goblins were looking for
them, too.

"We'll see you later then, girls," Rachel's
mum said with a smile. "Have fun!"

The four adults set off towards the
arboretum, with Buttons racing excitedly
ahead of them. Meanwhile, Rachel and
Kirsty headed down a different track
towards Rainbow Falls.

Just as they were walking past a path
that led to the orchid garden, Kirsty heard
a nasty chuckle.

"Did you hear that?" she whispered to Rachel. "It sounded like a goblin."

Rachel nodded. "Let's have a look in the orchid garden," she whispered.

The girls crept down the path to the orchid garden, looking carefully all around them. Goblins always meant trouble! And this time, Jack Frost had armed them with a wand of his own icy magic, which meant

they were far more powerful than usual.

It was quiet in the small, sheltered orchid garden, and neither Rachel nor Kirsty could see anyone else in there, only the gorgeous, colourful orchids blossoming everywhere. There were yellow, purple, pink and orange ones blooming from nooks and crannies all over the flowerbeds. Some orchids were even growing from tree stumps and logs!

"Wow," Kirsty breathed. "They're gorgeous!" Rachel was looking thoughtful. "Almost too gorgeous," she pointed out in a low voice. "The Orchid Petal's been stolen, so they should all be wilting."

Kirsty nodded. "The Orchid Petal must be nearby," she agreed. "It's the only thing that could be making these orchids so bright and healthy."

The girls knew that each of the seven magical petals helped a particular group of flowers to grow well. So the magical Orchid Petal made orchids bloom all

over the world, but it also ensured
that purple and blue flowers grew
healthily, too.

Kirsty's eyes widened as she caught
sight of a sudden movement in the
flowers. Something was rummaging
through the orchids! She elbowed Rachel
nervously as she spotted a familiar flash
of green.

"There's a goblin!" she hissed.

Goblins in the Garden

"Look, another one!" Rachel whispered, pointing to a second goblin on the other side of the garden. "And there are two more!"

"They must be searching for the Orchid Petal," Kirsty said.

"Well then, we'll have to look for it as well," Rachel declared. "We've got to find it before they do!"

The two girls crouched down and began peering into the flowerbeds, hoping to find the magic Orchid Petal, before the goblins noticed them. They hadn't been looking for very long, though, when they heard a triumphant goblin cry.

"I've got it! I've got it!"

Rachel and Kirsty looked up in dismay to see a goblin not far from them leaping up and down excitedly and waving a purple and blue petal in one hand.

"The Orchid Petal!" Kirsty groaned
as he raced off towards his friends.

The girls jumped to their feet as the
goblin ran across the garden. A large
raised flowerbed was in his path, and
he attempted to hurdle it, but he tripped
and fell into a patch of mud instead.

Rachel grabbed Kirsty's hand.
"Come on," she called. "Let's try
and get that petal!"

The girls hurried over to the goblin and stood over him.

"The fairies will be really cross with you if you don't give that back," Kirsty warned. "And Olivia the Orchid Fairy is probably on her way here right now!"

The goblin sat up and brushed the mud off himself, then he stuck his tongue out rudely. "Don't care!" he retorted, clutching the petal.

24

Just then, the air seemed
to shimmer around
them, and a tiny
fairy darted
into view.

Rachel smiled.
"Olivia!" she cried.

Olivia the Orchid
Fairy fluttered in
mid-air. She had glossy
dark hair, pulled back in a ponytail,
and a purple dress with bell sleeves and
a wide yellow belt. "Hello, girls," she
sang. "I see you've found my petal."

The goblin with the petal stood up
and backed away. "Uh-oh," he
murmured nervously. Then he spotted
his friends across the garden. "Hey!" he
shouted to them. "Help!"

Six other goblins rushed over. Kirsty noticed that one of them, a goblin with extremely large feet, was carrying the magic wand.

"The Orchid Petal is mine," Olivia told the goblins. "And I'd like it back please."

"Come any nearer, fairy, and I'll turn you into an ice cube," the goblin with the wand threatened. "Run!" he ordered his friends, and they took off across the garden as fast as they could go.

Then the goblin with the wand grinned and pulled a rude face. "You'll never see that petal again," he told the girls. "Never!" And with that he laughed nastily and went racing out of the garden at top speed.

Rainbows, Rainbows Everywhere!

"Quick! After them!" Kirsty shouted, streaking along the path with Rachel close behind.

Olivia zoomed through the air alongside them. "It'll be quicker if we all fly," she said, pointing her wand at the girls. A sparkling stream of purple and blue fairy dust swirled around

Kirsty and Rachel, immediately turning them into fairies.

"Thanks, Olivia," Rachel said, flapping her gauzy wings in delight. "Now let's catch up with those goblins."

The three friends flew through the air after the racing green figures. They were beginning to gain on the goblins when they rounded the corner and gasped to see Rainbow Falls ahead of them. A spectacular cascade of water plunged from high rocks into a large, deep pool just in front of the goblins, and the fine spray from the waterfall was making rainbows shimmer and dance in the air above the wet rocks that scattered the pool. The girls hovered in mid-air, gazing at the sight in wonder. There were signs all around the falls warning that the rocks were slippery so nobody should climb on them.

But the naughty goblins ignored all
these, and started clambering onto the
nearest rock.

"They're not going in the pool,
surely," Kirsty said in surprise. "Goblins
hate getting their feet wet!"

"They're using the rocks as stepping
stones," Rachel realised. "They're
determined to get away with that petal."

Olivia sighed. "Come on, let's follow
them," she said, and
the three girls
fluttered after
the goblins.
"You know,
all these
little rainbows
remind me of
the ones we've

used to travel to Fairyland," Kirsty said chattily. Then she smiled as an idea struck her. "You know, I've just thought of something that might stop those goblins!" she said to her friends in a low voice. "Just go along with what I say, OK?"

Rachel and Olivia nodded, looking curious.

Kirsty winked at them and then said loudly, "How lucky that the goblins have come to Rainbow Falls! Do you think they've noticed that these little rainbows are just like the magical rainbow bridges the Fairy King and Queen use to bring people to the Fairyland Palace?"

Rachel tried to hide a smile as she realised what her friend was up to. Clever Kirsty was trying to trick the goblins! Olivia seemed to have caught on, too, because she was agreeing loudly.

"Yes, they're exactly like the rainbow bridges," she said. "And a rainbow bridge could whisk you straight to the Fairy King and Queen if you stepped into one!"

Rachel nudged Kirsty with glee. It was obvious that the goblins had heard what the girls had been saying because they were looking extremely nervous on their stepping stones. They huddled together, muttering anxiously about being whisked off to answer to the King and Queen of Fairyland.

A rainbow formed right over the head of one goblin, and he drew back from it. "No! I don't want to go to Fairyland!" he exclaimed.

A second rainbow appeared near
the goblin with the Orchid Petal. "Nor
me. No way!" he yelped, hopping to
a different stone.

Then the goblin holding the wand let
out a shrill squeal as a rainbow
appeared right in front of his face.
"Ooh! I don't like this!" he wailed.

Kirsty and Rachel looked at one another. "They're so twitchy; they're not thinking about the petal at all now," Kirsty whispered.

Rachel nodded. "This might be a good chance for us to make a grab for it," she suggested.

"Good thinking," Olivia agreed. "If we all swoop down together, hopefully we'll catch them by surprise and we can get my petal back."

"Let's try," Kirsty said, looking determined. "One, two, three...GO!"

Ice Falls

The three fairies zoomed towards the goblins but, unfortunately, the goblins saw them coming.

"Oh, no, you don't!" one shouted, splashing water at the girls.

Kirsty dodged the spray, but Rachel wasn't so quick, and her wings became heavy with water. She shook them out,

and backed away, trying to flap
them dry.

Laughing, the goblins flicked more
water at the fairies, until all three of
them were forced to back off.

"That's right, fly away," the goblin
with the wand sneered. He put his
hands on his hips, but then jumped as
another rainbow appeared right by one

of his elbows. "Stupid rainbows! They're really getting on my nerves!" he snapped.

But the goblin with the petal was looking thoughtful. "How do we know these rainbows are magic, anyway?" he said. "What if those fairies are trying to trick us, like they did with the Sunflower Petal yesterday?"

Kirsty and Rachel exchanged a worried glance. Would the goblins realise that the rainbows were actually completely harmless?

"Why don't you step into one of them, if you think it's all a trick?" a skinny goblin challenged.

"Why should I do it?" the goblin with the petal replied. "You try it!" And he gave the skinny goblin a shove towards the nearest rainbow.

"Oi!" yelled the skinny goblin, falling

straight through the rainbow and into the pool with a splash. "Hey! It's freezing in here!" he shouted, struggling to clamber out. The other goblins ignored his complaints.

They were far too excited about
the discovery that the girls had
tricked them.

"Those rainbows aren't magic at all!"
one of them yelled, looking triumphant.

The goblin with the wand pulled the
skinny goblin out of the water, then
glared up at the fairies. "It's time to
sort those tricksy
fairies out once
and for all,"
he declared,
pointing
the wand
at them.
"This spell
will freeze you
into ice, no more
fairies, won't that be nice?" he shouted.

"Quick!" yelled Rachel. "Fly away!"

Three icy jets of magic poured from the wand towards the girls and Olivia. Hearts pounding, Kirsty and Rachel zoomed away from the freezing magic, with Olivia whizzing alongside.

The ice jets missed the three friends by a whisker and struck Rainbow Falls instead. Kirsty, Rachel and Olivia

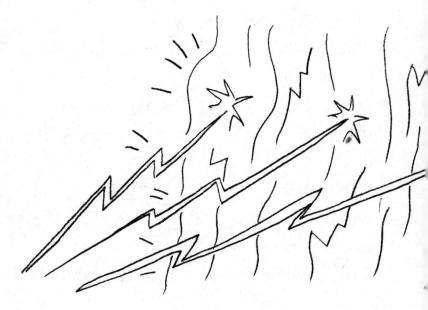

stopped and stared in amazement as
the entire waterfall and the pool below
were turned to solid ice, and the roar of
the water was silenced immediately.

"Wow!" Kirsty gulped. "It's beautiful!"

Even the goblins seemed transfixed by
the icy waterfall. The magic had frozen
every drop of water in an instant.

Even the fountains of spray were frozen in mid-air, like twinkling diamonds on a chandelier.

A shout from one of the goblins broke the silence. "Hey, we can walk across the pool now!"

Rachel looked down to see that the goblins were skidding and sliding across the ice. "They're heading around the back of the waterfall," she said. "Let's follow them."

The three fairies flew after the goblins, who had now slithered into the icy cave behind the

frozen waterfall. Kirsty, Rachel and
Olivia swooped into the cave after
them, swerving to avoid the gleaming
icicles that now hung from its roof.

"Where are they? Which way did
they go?" Rachel asked, looking around
the ice cave and seeing no sign of
the goblins.

The water had frozen into unusual
twisted shapes, rather like
crystal sculptures, and the
sun shone through
them, making them
glitter and sparkle
with a bright,
white light. "It's
so beautiful,"
Kirsty said,
wide-eyed.
"Like a magical
ice world."

Rachel nodded.
"It's a bit like
a frozen Fairyland,"
she said in awe, "all
glittery and sparkly. But there
isn't a goblin in sight."

"We'll have to search for them,"
Olivia said. "They must be
here somewhere."
The three friends
fluttered around the
cave, peering
behind the
strange ice
formations
in search of
the goblins.
"There are so
many places the
goblins could
hide," Kirsty sighed,
seeing pathways
leading away from the
back of the cave. "It's like
a maze in here!"

Just then, Rachel let out a cry. "Look, there's a flower!" she called, pointing to the icy wall on her left.

Kirsty and Olivia fluttered over to see a bright purple orchid blooming right out of the ice.

"Only my petal could have done that," Olivia said, looking excited. "Orchids take a long time and lots of love to grow that big!"

Kirsty's face lit up as she saw another orchid, an orange one this time, further down the cave wall. She pointed to it delightedly. "It's a trail of flowers!" she cried. "The goblins must have gone this way!"

Flower Trail

The three friends followed the trail of orchids along the passage. Then Olivia swooped in front of Kirsty and Rachel, motioning for them to stop. "I can hear the goblins whispering ahead," she said in a low voice. "We mustn't be seen. They might try to turn us into ice again!"

Rachel and Kirsty nodded. They
certainly didn't like the idea of being
frozen solid, like the waterfall.

The three of them cautiously flew
a little further, Olivia leading the way,
until they came to the edge of an ice
chamber. Very carefully, Rachel peeped
around the block of ice that stood at
the entrance, to see a row of icicles
dangling from the ceiling, and the
goblins all huddled in a narrow crevice.

"I'm f-f-f-freezing," one of them moaned, his teeth chattering.

"It's colder than Jack Frost's Ice Castle in here," another agreed, wrapping his arms around himself.

The goblin with the Orchid Petal was the only one who didn't seem to be bothered by the cold. He was amusing himself by dragging the magic petal along the icy walls, making bright new orchids bloom everywhere.

Drip!

A drop of water fell from an icicle onto a goblin's head. "Who's dripping water on me?" he spluttered.

"Be quiet! Those fairies will hear you!" another scolded him. "Nobody's dripping water on you," a third told him crossly. "Don't be stupid!"

"Olivia, could you turn us back into girls now?" Kirsty asked in a whisper, as the goblins continued to bicker. "We'll have more chance of getting the Orchid Petal that way, I think."

"Of course," Olivia said, waving her
wand over the girls. A stream of purple
and blue fairy dust poured from the tip
of the wand, and floated around Kirsty
and Rachel.

Rachel shivered, as she became a girl
once more. It felt even colder in here
now that she was standing still, rather
than zipping around on her fairy wings.

57

Her teeth began to chatter, but luckily, before the goblins could notice the sound, there came yells from two more goblins who had been dripped on by icicles.

"The magic spell is wearing off," Kirsty realised. "The ice is melting!"

Drip! Drip! Drip!

"Whose idea was it to sit here, anyway?" the goblin with the wand complained, as freezing water ran down his back. "Let's get out of here!"

Rachel and Kirsty stepped in front of the goblins as they got up to leave the chamber. "Not before you give us that magic petal," Rachel said bravely.

The goblins all shook their heads. "There's no way we're going back to Jack Frost without this petal," the one with the wand said. "We're keeping it, and that's that!"

"But haven't you realised that your spell is fading?" Kirsty pointed out. "You can't stay here. Soon, the waterfall will have melted completely!"

"And we are right in the middle of it," Rachel added, "so when all the ice melts, we'll be thrown against the rocks by the water!" She shuddered at the thought, hoping that the goblins would realise how dangerous the situation was and see sense!

Drip! Drip! Drip! Drip!

The goblins looked around nervously, as the drops of water started falling faster. "Let us out!" the skinny one cried, trying to push past the girls. "Give us the petal first," Rachel countered, standing firm.

The goblin with the wand pointed it threateningly at the girls, but Olivia let out a tinkling laugh. "Your spell didn't work very well last time, did it?" she reminded him.

"She's right," the skinny goblin muttered, pushing his friend's wand down again. "No more magic!"

By now, the drips had turned into little streams, soaking the goblins. "Ugh!" they cried, trying to shield their heads with their arms.

Kirsty and Rachel were getting
wet, too.

"We're running out of time," Kirsty
said, looking around at the ice chamber
as water streamed down its walls.
"This place is melting fast!"

"You don't really want to end up in
the middle of a waterfall, do you?"
Rachel asked.

"No!" the goblins wailed miserably.
"Let us out!"

Rachel shook her head firmly as melted
ice started to pour down in the chamber
like rain. In despair,
the goblin with the
petal shoved it into
Rachel's hands
and then
barged past her.

"We give up, you win!" he moaned, running back the way he'd come.

"Let's get out of here!" shouted another goblin, and all six of the remaining goblins raced after their friend.

Olivia beamed to see her petal safely in Rachel's hands. "Well done, girls!" she cried thankfully, shrinking the petal to its Fairyland size with a wave of her wand.

"The ice is melting quickly now," Kirsty said. "I think we should get out of here."

Rachel nodded, then gasped as a huge chunk of the icy ceiling gave way with a crash. "We've only got a few seconds left," she cried. "Run!"

Purple Perfection

"We'll fly out," Olivia called, waving her wand over the girls. "It's quicker."

Kirsty, who'd been slipping and sliding along the slushy ice floor, suddenly felt as light as air, as she turned into a fairy again. She flapped her wings gratefully. "Let's go!" she shouted.

The three friends zoomed out of the fast-melting waterfall at top speed, and darted out from beneath the icy cascade at the entrance in the nick of time. As they turned to look back, hovering safely in mid-air, there came a great cracking sound and the ice split clean apart. As it broke, water began cascading freely over the falls once

more, tumbling and crashing into the pool below.

"That was close!" Kirsty breathed, as the waterfall's roar started up again. "Thanks, Olivia. I don't think I've ever been so glad to have fairy wings."

Rachel grinned. "Look, there go the goblins," she said, watching as they grumpily trudged off into the woods.

Olivia gazed at her Orchid Petal happily. "Thank you so much, girls, I couldn't have got this back without you," she said. "And now I should take it back to Fairyland where it belongs. Once it's there, I can use its magic to help all the orchids and the blue and purple flowers to grow properly again."

Kirsty checked her watch.

"And it's time for us to go and meet our mums and dads," she said. "I bet they haven't had half as much fun as we have!"

"I'll speed you on your way with a last bit of fairy magic if you like," Olivia offered. "You'll be girls again, when you arrive."

"Oh, thank you," Rachel said eagerly. She did so love fairy magic!

Olivia hugged them goodbye and then waved her wand over them. Immediately, the girls were surrounded by a cloud of glittering blue and purple fairy dust. When it cleared, a moment later, they found themselves at the entrance to the arboretum, where they were due to meet their parents.

As the last few sparkles vanished at their feet, Kirsty caught sight of her parents strolling along the path to meet them. "Just in time!" she giggled under her breath to Rachel.

Rachel laughed, then waved at her mum and dad. "Hello! How was the arboretum?" she called, bending down to pat Buttons who had bounded excitedly over to her. Mr Walker looked disappointed. "Well, it wasn't quite as spectacular as I'd hoped," he replied.

"I thought the lilac trees would be flowering by now, but there wasn't a single blossom."

Rachel glanced at Kirsty, guessing it was because the Orchid Petal had been missing. Hopefully, Olivia would be back in Fairyland with it soon, and then the blue and purple flowers – including the lilacs – would start bursting into bloom.

"We spotted a nice-looking café where we can go for lunch, though," Mrs Tate said. "It's just inside the arboretum."

"That sounds great," Kirsty smiled. "I'm starving!"

The two families began walking through the arboretum towards the restaurant. As they did so, Rachel and Kirsty spotted several flowering lilac trees and a wonderful purple climbing flower that was rambling

all over an old brick wall.

"Look! The lilacs are blooming here!"
Mr Tate said in astonishment.

"And that clematis is wonderful,"
Mr Walker said, pointing at the flowers
on the wall. "I can't believe we didn't
notice it before."

Rachel and Kirsty grinned at each other as they walked along. Olivia's Orchid Petal was already working its magic with beautiful results.

"Hurrah for Petal Magic!" Rachel said in a whisper.

Kirsty nodded, smiling. "That's five petals we've helped send safely back to Fairyland," she said happily. "I hope we can find the other two before our holiday is over."

RAINBOW magic®

The Petal Fairies

Olivia the Orchid Fairy has got her magic petal back. Now Rachel and Kirsty must help

Danielle the Daisy Fairy

TIA THE TULIP FAIRY
978-1-84616-457-6

PIPPA THE POPPY FAIRY
978-1-84616-458-3

LOUISE THE LILY FAIRY
978-1-84616-459-0

CHARLOTTE THE
SUNFLOWER FAIRY
978-1-84616-460-6

OLIVIA THE ORCHID FAIRY
978-1-84616-461-3

DANIELLE THE DAISY FAIRY
978-1-84616-462-0

ELLA THE ROSE FAIRY
978-1-84616-464-4

Win Rainbow Magic goodies!

In every book in the Rainbow Magic Petal Fairies series (books 43-49) there is a hidden picture of a petal with a secret letter in it. Find all seven letters and re-arrange them to make a special Petal Fairies word, then send it to us. Each month we will put the entries into a draw and select one winner to receive a Rainbow Magic Sparkly T-shirt and Goody Bag!

Send your entry on a postcard to Rainbow Magic Fun Day Competition, Orchard Books, 338 Euston Road, London NW1 3BH. Australian readers should write to Hachette Children's Books, Level 17/207 Kent Street, Sydney, NSW 2000. New Zealand readers should write to Rainbow Magic Competition, 4 Whetu Place, Mairangi Bay, Auckland, NZ. Don't forget to include your name and address. Only one entry per child. Final draw: 30th April 2008.

Good luck!

Have you checked out the

website at:
www.rainbowmagic.co.uk

RAINBOW magic®

by Daisy Meadows

The Pet Keeper Fairies

Katie the Kitten Fairy	ISBN	978 1 84616 166 7
Bella the Bunny Fairy	ISBN	978 1 84616 170 4
Georgia the Guinea Pig Fairy	ISBN	978 1 84616 168 1
Lauren the Puppy Fairy	ISBN	978 1 84616 169 8
Harriet the Hamster Fairy	ISBN	978 1 84616 167 4
Molly the Goldfish Fairy	ISBN	978 1 84616 172 8
Penny the Pony Fairy	ISBN	978 1 84616 171 1

The Fun Day Fairies

Megan the Monday Fairy	ISBN	978 184616 188 9
Tallulah the Tuesday Fairy	ISBN	978 1 84616 189 6
Willow the Wednesday Fairy	ISBN	978 1 84616 190 2
Thea the Thursday Fairy	ISBN	978 1 84616 191 9
Freya the Friday Fairy	ISBN	978 1 84616 192 6
Sienna the Saturday Fairy	ISBN	978 1 84616 193 3
Sarah the Sunday Fairy	ISBN	978 1 84616 194 0

Holly the Christmas Fairy	ISBN	978 1 84362 661 9
Summer the Holiday Fairy	ISBN	978 1 84362 960 3
Stella the Star Fairy	ISBN	978 1 84362 869 9
Kylie the Carnival Fairy	ISBN	978 1 84616 175 9
Paige the Pantomime Fairy	ISBN	978 1 84616 047 9
The Rainbow Magic Treasury	ISBN	978 1 84616 209 1

Coming soon:

Flora the Fancy Dress Fairy	ISBN	978 1 84616 505 4

All priced at £3.99. *Holly the Christmas Fairy, Summer the Holiday Fairy, Stella the Star Fairy, Kylie the Carnival Fairy, Paige the Pantomime Fairy* and *Flora the Fancy Dress Fairy* are priced at £5.99. *The Rainbow Magic Treasury* is priced at £12.99.
Rainbow Magic books are available from all good bookshops, or can be ordered direct from the publisher: Orchard Books, PO BOX 29, Douglas IM99 1BQ
Credit card orders please telephone 01624 836000
or fax 01624 837033 or visit our Internet site: www.wattspub.co.uk
or e-mail: bookshop@enterprise.net for details.

To order please quote title, author and ISBN and your full name and address.
Cheques and postal orders should be made payable to 'Bookpost plc.'
Postage and packing is FREE within the UK
(overseas customers should add £2.00 per book).
Prices and availability are subject to change.

Look out for the Dance Fairies!

BETHANY
THE BALLET FAIRY
978-1-84616-490-3

JADE
THE DISCO FAIRY
978-1-84616-491-0

REBECCA
THE ROCK 'N' ROLL FAIRY
978-1-84616-492-7

TASHA
THE TAP DANCE FAIRY
978-1-84616-493-4

JESSICA
THE JAZZ FAIRY
978-1-84616-495-8

SASKIA
THE SALSA FAIRY
978-1-84616-496-5

IMOGEN
THE ICE DANCE FAIRY
978-1-84616-497-2

Available Now!